HOWIE
HELPS HIMSELF

Joan Fassler, Ph.D.

Illustrated by Joe Lasker

Albert Whitman & Company
Morton Grove, Illinois

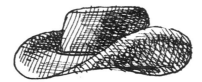

Joan Fassler is a faculty member and Research Associate at the Yale University Child Study Center, New Haven, Connecticut, where she works on two related topics, child development and children's literature. She has been associated with the Research and Demonstration Center for the Education of Handicapped Children, Columbia University, where she conducted studies with cerebral palsied and autistic children.

Joe Lasker is author and illustrator of the picture book He's My Brother *in which a child with a learning disability and his family are described. He is the illustrator of numerous picture books and an accomplished painter.*

The author expresses appreciation to Miss Dolma Laden-La, Senior Physical Therapist, Pediatric Division, Institute for Rehabilitation Medicine, New York City, for many helpful suggestions. Appreciation is also expressed by the illustrator to various staff members at the Institute for their kindness and cooperation which enabled him to observe selected classroom activities and rehabilitative procedures.

Library of Congress Cataloging-in-Publication Data

Fassler, Joan.
    Howie helps himself.
    Summary: Though he enjoys life with his family and attends school, Howie, a child with cerebral palsy, wants more than anything else to be able to move his wheelchair by himself.
    [1. Cerebral palsy—Fiction. 2. Physically handicapped—Fiction.] I. Lasker, Joe, illus. II. Title.
PZ7.F26Ho   [E]   74-12284
ISBN 0-8075-3422-6

About This Book . . .

This is a story of a child who is physically handicapped. Because of handicapping conditions, such as cerebral palsy, at least one out of ten school-aged children is in need of special help. Many of these children attend regular public schools. Others are in private day or residential schools, while some are educated at home.

At one time, the disabilities of such children were often hidden or denied. Today when possible, these children are included in public school classrooms, receiving whatever special services they may need (or are available) to reach their own optimum development.

This book, it is hoped, will be useful in several ways. First, a child in a wheelchair may find something special: the chance to identify with a picture-book child who happens to be handicapped. Siblings may find as they respond to Howie's story a welcome opportunity to share with interested and understanding adults some of the joys, stresses, and strains of being the sister or brother of a handicapped person.

This story also encourages the growth of positive attitudes on the part of normal children toward those who are handicapped. It is not unusual for young children to feel anxious and fearful when they see someone in a wheelchair. Becoming familiar with such a child and his equipment in a nonthreatening situation like a story shared together may reduce this anxiety. It thus helps normal children accept and be more open in their response to the handicapped.

Finally, this is a story to enjoy. It is about a boy whose emotions can be recognized by many children, no matter what their experience with handicaps has been. Howie is a person in his own right.

Howie is a boy with brown eyes
and brown hair and a soft, warm smile.

Howie likes to watch the snow fall.

He likes to eat chocolate ice cream.

He likes to ride in the car with his daddy.

But there are many things that Howie cannot do at all.

Howie's legs are weak, so he cannot run or skip or jump.

He cannot walk without something to hold onto. And even then, he cannot go very far or very fast.

He cannot ride a bike or climb a tree or chase a ball.

Howie's hands are weak, too.
He cannot hold a pencil well enough
to write his name.

He cannot hold a cup steady enough
to drink his milk.

And he cannot build a tower or a castle
with his wooden blocks—not even
a very little tower or a very small castle.

Howie lives in a big apartment building with
his mother, his father, and his sister Linda.

His mother helps Howie do many things he cannot
do by himself. Howie's father helps him, too.

Linda is great at playing games with Howie. Sometimes she puts a ball in Howie's lap, and he pushes it back to her again and again, until he gets tired or bored.

Sometimes Linda and Howie play picture dominoes. And sometimes Linda takes thick round crayons and draws things Howie especially likes.

But other times Linda is busy when Howie wants
to play. "I can't play now," she says. "Maybe later."

Then Howie puts his head down and feels sad.
Or else he gets mad. He grumbles and scowls.

Howie doesn't want to wait for later.
When he wants something, he wants it NOW!

On weekends, Howie's grandmother takes him
to the park.

Howie likes to play ball with his grandmother, too.
He pushes the ball out of his lap, and his grandmother
tries to catch it. Sometimes she misses.

Then Howie's grandmother has to chase after the ball.
Howie laughs and laughs. He thinks it's so funny
to see his little grandmother running down hill
as fast as she can after a big red ball.

Every weekday morning at nine o'clock
Howie goes to school.

He rides in a special bus and goes
to a special class.

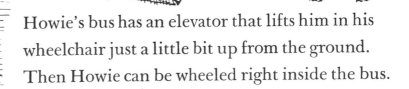

Howie's bus has an elevator that lifts him in his wheelchair just a little bit up from the ground. Then Howie can be wheeled right inside the bus.

Howie likes to ride up on the elevator. He smiles.

Most days, Howie likes school. He likes the other children. He likes his teachers.

He likes to keep busy and learn new things. And Howie does learn many things at school. There's a lot for him to learn.

He learns songs and games. He learns to read the letters of the alphabet. He learns to count with colored beads and wooden blocks. He learns to pronounce sounds and words.

And every day Howie does some exercises to help his arms and legs grow stronger.

Howie worked hard at school. He practiced some things
over and over until finally he knew how to do them.

But there was one special thing Howie wanted most to do.
It was his own special wish.

More than anything else, Howie wanted to zoom around in
his wheelchair without any help at all. He wanted to move
his wheelchair all by himself. Susan and Jeffrey could
already do that. But not Howie. He just couldn't.

For days and days, Howie had tried to move his wheelchair. He tried very hard.

But somehow he could not make the wheels turn.

His teachers helped him. "Push the wheels this way," they said. They showed him over and over. Still Howie couldn't do it, not even a little bit.

"It's not easy," one of his teachers said. "But soon you will learn how. Just keep practicing. Put your two hands on the wheels and try to turn them a little at a time. Don't give up."

And Howie did practice. He didn't give up. Not really. But sometimes he almost gave up.

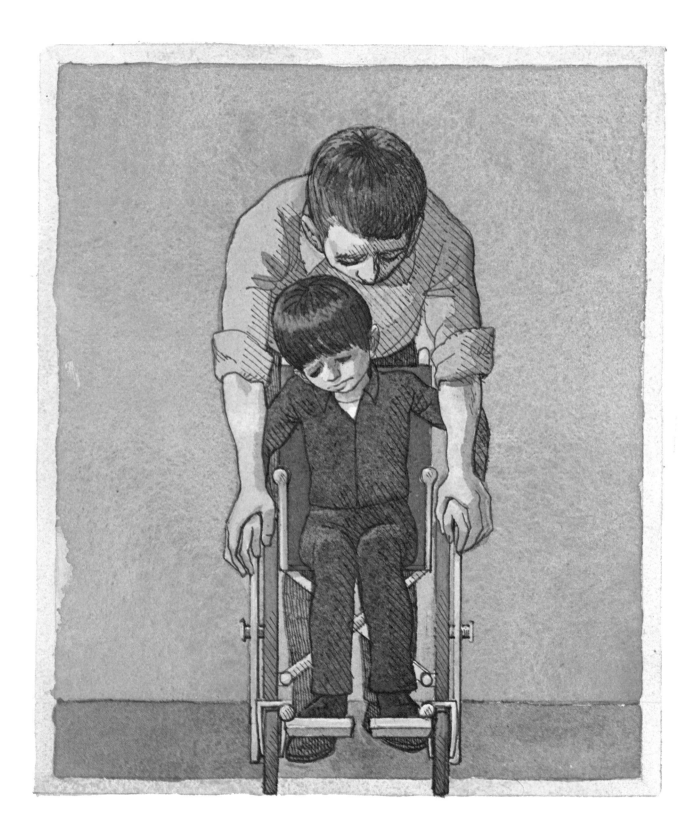

Not all school days were good for Howie.
Some days Howie didn't feel just right. Some
days he felt especially tired or angry or clumsy.

And on some days he felt like crying—and he did.
Quietly to himself.

Nothing would cheer him up.

Sometimes when the day was over Howie's daddy came to take him home from school.

One day, Howie had been feeling especially good. He had been busy that day—so busy that he did not know it was time to go home.

Howie looked up from his work. He saw his daddy standing in the doorway. Howie smiled.

Suddenly Howie's face became serious. He had a plan.
Howie took a deep breath. He lifted one hand very slowly
and placed it on one wheel of his wheelchair.

He lifted his other hand very slowly and placed it on
the other wheel of his wheelchair.

Then Howie moved one hand with a quick movement,
just as his teachers had shown him. He didn't stop.
He kept right on moving one hand until, little by little,
Howie turned his wheelchair around ALL BY HIMSELF.

Now he was facing his daddy, and that was exactly
what Howie wanted.

For a moment
Howie looked straight at his daddy.
Then he looked down at his wheelchair wheels.

Very quietly, very seriously, Howie began to push
hard on the two big wheels. Slowly the wheels
began to turn.

Howie pushed as hard as he possibly could. He
pushed so hard small drops of sweat ran down
his forehead. He pushed so hard his fingers
became white from all the effort.

Howie pushed and pushed until he thought
he just couldn't push those two big wheels
any more at all.

He was too tired.

Then Howie looked up—

He found he had pushed himself right up to his daddy!
That made Howie so happy his face became one great big smile.

Howie stretched up his arms as high as they would go until they
went right around his daddy's neck. And he hugged his daddy
just as tightly as he possibly could.

And do you know something? When a boy hugs his daddy, it
really doesn't make any difference how weak or strong the boy's
arms are. It's how the boy feels deep down inside himself that
really counts. And how his daddy feels, too.

And at that moment Howie and his daddy both felt very good inside.

Then Howie's daddy wheeled Howie's wheelchair out of the school and right up to his car.

When he reached the car, he tipped the wheelchair back a little. He wheeled it up a small ramp and inside the car.

Howie's daddy snapped each wheel tightly into place so that Howie would have a safe ride.

Then Howie's daddy stopped for a moment. He bent down and brushed some hair out of Howie's eyes. And he kissed Howie very gently on the forehead.

And Howie and his daddy drove home.